I dedicate this book to my parents, Barry and Gloria.

**www.mascotbooks.com**

©2012 Barry Jordan, Jr. All Rights Reserved. No part of this
publication may be reproduced, stored in a retrieval system
or transmitted in any form by any means electronic, mechanical,
or photocopying, recording or otherwise without the permission
of the author.

**For more information, please contact:**
Mascot Books
560 Herndon Parkway #120
Herndon, VA 20170
info@mascotbooks.com

Library of Congress Control Number: 2012948552

CPSIA Code: PRT1112A
ISBN: 1-62086-141-0
ISBN-13: 978-1-62086-141-7

Printed in the United States

"Boy, will you stop playing those video games and go with me to the store?"

"Off to the store! Off to the store we go, Boy," said Grandma. "Oh! What a joy."

"Wow! Look at this crowd in the pet store, Grandma," said Boy. "Can I get a dog?"

"Noooooooooooooooooooooooo!

That is not why we came to this store.

This store is more than a pet store.

Didn't you know that, Boy?"

Boy was puzzled, "Are you sure, Grandma?" asked Boy.

All I see are dogs, cats, birds, and frogs.

"That's crazy talk, Boy," said Grandma.

"Don't you see these biscuits over here?

They sell all types of food.

Here, try one, Boy!"

"That's okay. I'm not hungry right

now, Grandma," said Boy.

"How do you like these shirts over here?" said Grandma. "You need to try one on. They're one size fits all."

"Grandma, it doesn't fit!" said Boy.

"Hmmm, they must be irregular.

Oh, well, it's your loss, Boy," said Grandma.

"What! What was that?" responded Grandma.

"Oh wow! Look at the dogs!" yelled Boy.

"Grandma, please, please, can I get a dog?"

"No, no, noooo! You cannot get a dog!" said Grandma. "It's just way too much responsibility. You will not walk him, talk to him, or even throw him a bone. So no, Boy, you cannot get a dog."

*Ring, ring, ring,* sounded the alarm on the cashier's register.

Lights started flashing, confetti started to fall, and balloons came flying down. "Congratulations, you are the customer of the day!" said the cashier. "You have just won a new dog!"

"Awesome!" said Boy.

"Nooo!" said Grandma who was having a fit. She caused such an uproar in the store as she yelled at the top of her lungs.

A sales lady walked the dog to them.

"Grandma, can I keep the dog?

I will take good care of him."

As Boy stood in the middle of the pet store, every worker and shopper waited for Grandma's response.

When Grandma saw the dog, her frown turned into a smile.

"Yes, yes, yes! You can keep the dog!"

said Grandma.

# About the Author

Barry G. Jordan Jr. was born in San Antonio, Texas. At age five, his family moved to Chesapeake, Virginia. He always took an interest in reading. As a young child, he received a certificate for participating in the Young Readers Program from the Virginia State Reading Association. Barry also had a talent and a love for art. In third grade, he entered a drawing in the Keep Chesapeake Clean and Green Poster Contest and won third place. He continued doing well throughout his school years at Indian River High School. Barry majored in Art at Norfolk State University, graduating with a Bachelor of Arts in Fine Arts/Graphic Design.